☆ ☆ ☆

Here's what some lovely people have said about me!

'Made me laugh out loud. Ellie May rocks!' Andy Stanton, author of *Mr Gum*

'A playful poke at the fame game . . . packed with wit and lively illustrations.'
Independent on Sunday

'I loved Ellie May. There wasn't a page I didn't like – it was sooooooo good!' Imogen, age 9

'Superbly quirky and amusing.' Konnie Huq (Blue Peter, The Xtra Factor)

'I thought this book was amazing and a real page-turner.' Grace, age 8

'Move over, Clarice Bean! A wonderful read for young fashionistas!' *Carousel*

'OMG, here comes Ellie May! She had me choking on my fudge cake with laughter!' Mel Giedroyc (The Great British Bake Off)

'Plenty of laugh-out-loud moments. Ellie May is a heroine with attitude a go-go.' *Ham & High*

'I would like Ellie May to come to my school and be my best friend. One time I giggled so much reading it I fell out of bed!' Elsie, age 7

'Ellie May is very funny. This is seriously the best book I've ever read!' Poppy, age 8

'Vivacious and hilarious.' *The Bookseller*

'I loved this book more than fudge cake.' Freya, age 8

'Girls will love this new heroine and laugh out loud at her antics.'
Angels and Urchins

'Fast, daft and funny. You're guaranteed unalloyed hilarity!'
Kids Confidential

☆ ☆ ☆ ☆ ☆

To E.A.D. and J.D.F. with gratitude

EGMONT

We bring stories to life

Ellie May Would Like to be
Taken Seriously for a Change
First published in paperback in Great Britain
2012 by Jelly Pie, an imprint of
Egmont UK Limited
This edition published in 2014
by Egmont UK Limited,
The Yellow Building,
1 Nicholas Road, London W11 4AN

Text copyright © 2012 Marianne Levy
Illustrations copyright © 2012 Ali Pye

The moral rights of the author and illustrator
have been asserted

ISBN 978 0 6035 7084 1

www.egmont.co.uk
www.jellypiecentral.com

A CIP catalogue record for this title is
available from the British Library

58525/1

Printed in the United Kingdom

EGMONT

Would Like to be Taken Seriously for a Change

Marianne Levy

EGMONT

Contents

Chapter One

Ellie May Would Like to be Taken Seriously for a Change

Ellie May was an incredibly famous film star.

Not one of those film stars who was a little bit famous, where people would say, 'Ellie May. We know that name from somewhere. Has she been on television, then?'

No, Ellie May was the kind of film star where people would say, 'Ellie May! Of course we know who you mean! She's that incredibly famous film star!'

In the last year, for example, she'd starred in *Tears Before Bedtime*, *The Darkest Night* and *Flufflepuffs: The Movie!*

She'd been shopping in Paris, shopping in London, and over to LA for some interviews, and to do a bit of shopping.

She'd collected a BRA award, for 'Best Recent Appearance', and a CAFE, a 'Critics' Award for Excellence'. Best of all, she had just been nominated for *Giggle* magazine's 'Seriously And Unbelievably Stunningly Amazingest Girl Ever!' award, otherwise known as a SAUSAGE.

And right now she was about to finish her latest film, *Alien Attack*. In fact, there was just one line left to say:

'*Now the aliens are gone, and the world will be safe forever!*'

'Cut!' called the director. 'And that's a wrap. We're finished! Well done, everybody!'

The cameraman switched off his camera, the sound man put down his microphone and the stuntman stopped crashing his car into a wall and started eating an ice cream.

'Thanks, Ellie May,' said the director, as she folded up her director's chair. 'You've been wonderful, as always.'

'It's been amazingly amazing,' said Ellie May.

☆ 4 ☆

'Are you coming to the premiere? What do you think you'll wear? I haven't decided yet. I've got this brilliant pair of shoes I found in New York. They're pink with silver bows on them and they're absolutely perfect. Except that I'm not totally sure about the bows. Or the pink. It might not go with my hair. But then, my feet are quite far away from my hair. Hmm.'

Like the rest of her, Ellie May's hair was incredibly famous. Practically everyone in the world knew that it was long and red, and that her eyes were big and green. Her fingernails were notedly nibbled, her knees notedly knobbly.

And she smelled of strawberry lipgloss, but not many people knew that.

'Oh, Ellie May,' said the director. 'You do know that this premiere is about our film, and not just your shoes, don't you?'

'It is mainly about the film,' said Ellie May. 'But I think we all know that it is a little bit about my shoes as well.'

'Honestly! It's lucky you're not a grown-up, or I'd have things to say to you!' laughed the director. 'And it's been nice working with you too, Jeffrey. This was your first time chaperoning Ellie May, wasn't it? I hope you've enjoyed it.'

⭐ 6 ⭐

'Well,' said Jeffrey, a small, neat, worried young man with a round, worried face, a worried little mouth and curly, worried hair. 'I have to say, it was all a bit worrying, especially at the beginning. Ellie May's so incredibly famous, you see, and film sets are enormous – I'd never been on one before, and –'

'Well, we've certainly loved having you,' said the director. 'Fudge cake, whenever we want it! And I don't think I've ever met anyone your age with such an enormous collection of bow ties.'

'Yes,' said the stuntman. 'You and Ellie May do look funny together.'

'What do you mean?' asked Jeffrey, shifting nervously in his tweedy jacket. 'The sort of funny that makes you laugh, or the sort of funny that just means strange?'

'Both!' said the stuntman. 'Would you like some of my ice cream?'

'Never mind ice cream,' said Ellie May. 'It's tea time, and I want some fudge cake. Bye, everyone!'

'Bye!' called the director.

'Bye!' called the stuntman.

'Oh dear,' muttered Jeffrey.

Ellie May had to spend lots of time in her trailer when she was working, so she always liked to personalise it with souvenirs from her previous films. From *Cushion My Fall*, she had acquired some gorgeous pink cushions, from *Sofa Surfer*, a beautiful purple sofa. And from her international blockbuster *Mirror Lake*, Ellie May had managed to keep a full-sized canoe.

Now she flumped down on to the sofa, looked at her feet and sighed.

'Jeffrey,' said Ellie May. 'There's nothing wrong with me liking shoes, is there?'

'What?' said Jeffrey, who wasn't really listening.

'Oh, nothing,' said Ellie May.

'Ellie May,' said Jeffrey. 'There's nothing wrong with the way I dress, is there?'

'What?' said Ellie May, who wasn't really listening.

'Oh, nothing,' said Jeffrey.

'Are you all right?' asked Ellie May. 'What are you worrying about now? It's the end of the film! Let's celebrate!'

Jeffrey shook himself. 'Yes,' he said. 'We should celebrate. Would you like a treat?'

'Yes!' cried Ellie May. 'I would like a treat! What is it what is it what is it? Wait, let's make it a game. Is it . . . something to do with antelopes?'

'I think I'm going to tell you, if that's all right,' said Jeffrey, who had played guessing games with Ellie May before and knew how long they could take. 'It's the new edition of *Giggle*.'

'*Giggle?*' cried Ellie May. 'That's only my favourite magazine in the whole entire universe! They've nominated me for their SAUSAGE award, Jeffrey, did I tell you?'

'You did, yes,' said Jeffrey.

'Look! They call me "Film's Most Fashionable Star". And I'm on the cover! Amazing!' Ellie May flicked from page to page. 'There's an article all about eyeshadow. There's a page about having long hair. I've got long hair! And there's an interview with Cassie Craven.'

Cassie Craven's Got ☆ A Serious Side!

● ● ● ● ● ● ● ● ● ● ● ● ● ● ● ●

The SAUSAGE-nominated young lady is a very different person from the carefree girl we met a few months ago.

'I had a lot of letters from my fans about the dolphins,' Cassie told us, brushing away a tear. 'They're in trouble. Real trouble. So from now on I'm going to do everything I can to save them.'

14

∞ There is a time to giggle, and a time to be serious ∞

This dedicated actress has even taken time off between films to campaign for the dolphins. 'I'm going to be speaking out about their plight,' she told us, 'and I'm hoping to go swimming with them, too.'

Is Cassie our Seriously And Unbelievably Stunningly Amazingest Girl Ever? We're not telling! But, as she herself says, 'There is a time to giggle, and a time to be serious. Life's not all about clothes and handbags, you know . . .'

'What a nice girl!' said Jeffrey. 'And look, here's your interview!' He turned the page to reveal the headline:

Life's All About Clothes And Handbags Says Ellie May!

Ellie May closed the magazine. 'That does it,' she said.

'What does what?' asked Jeffrey.

'People think I only care about clothes and shoes and handbags. When actually I care about a lot of things!'

'Do you?' asked Jeffrey.

'And now you too! I'm not the shallow person you all think I am and I would like to be taken seriously for a change.'

'I never said you were shallow!' said Jeffrey.

'How am I supposed to be *Giggle*'s Seriously And Unbelievably Stunningly Amazingest Girl Ever if they don't take me seriously?' howled Ellie May. 'Without the Seriously it's just an AUSAGE. And that's not even a proper word. Is it? No. Or is it?'

'Calm down,' said Jeffrey. 'I know you care

about a lot of things. And I'm sure the reporters at *Giggle* know it too.'

'Dolphins!' cried Ellie May. 'I care about the dolphins. Dolphins are nice. They're my favourite fish, except maybe whatever the ones are that they make into sushi. I'm going to save the dolphins! Then everyone will take me seriously.'

'Or you could try saving something else,' said Jeffrey.

Ellie May gave him a look.

'I just wonder if some people might think you're copying Cassie,' he said. 'Silly people. Who don't know what they're talking about.'

'All right, all right,' said Ellie May. 'Well, Cassie said she'd had lots of letters from her fans. So maybe my fans will have written to me about something that needs saving. Can I look at my fan mail please, Jeffrey?'

Jeffrey trotted into the next room and returned with an enormous armful of letters, which he emptied all over the carpet. 'This week's fan mail,' he said. 'I'm sure there'll be lots of letters here about saving things. Lots and lots and lots.'

Ellie May sat down on the floor and began to read.

Dear Ellie May

I have to buy a new dress for my birthday party. What colour do you think I should get?

'Oh,' said Ellie May.

Dear Ellie May

I want to start wearing perfume! What perfume do you wear?

'Ah,' said Ellie May.

'Let me help,' said Jeffrey, sitting down next to her. 'Here's one about saving! Hang on . . .'

'Well? What does it say?' cried Ellie May.

'No,' said Jeffrey. 'No, no, no. A girl called Jess wants to know whether it's worth saving up pocket money to buy expensive nail varnish. Not what you mean at all.'

'You're right, it isn't,' said Ellie May, leaning over to see Jess's letter, which was actually asking a very difficult and interesting question. She tucked it into her pocket for later, and reached for the next envelope.

Ellie May clambered dejectedly to her feet. 'Would you like a cup of tea, Jeffrey? I think I'm going to stop, just for a minute, and make us both a cup of tea.'

'All right,' said Jeffrey. 'If you're having one.'

'Where's my special pink mug?' asked Ellie May. 'Oh. I remember. I broke it last week. I suppose I'll just have to have the blue one.' She sighed. 'It doesn't really matter.'

Jeffrey stood and turned to Ellie May as she clattered about by the kettle. 'Now, you must cheer up,' he said. 'We'll fly back to England tomorrow and stay in a fun hotel, and you can swim in the pool and get facials. And if you're very good I'll let you have cake for breakfast.'

'Will you have some too?' snuffled Ellie May.

'A little bit, maybe,' said Jeffrey, who wasn't really a cake-for-breakfast sort of a person. 'And then it's your premiere. You can get all dressed up!'

'All dressed up,' sighed Ellie May, passing Jeffrey his mug and settling back down on the carpet. 'I'll just read one more letter,' she said. 'One more.'

Dear Ellie May

I have seen your picture on the front of magazines and I think you look a bit funny but maybe underneath you are all right.

My name is Lettice and I live in Newton Bingley. There is a nature reserve at my school full of insects and plants. Soon it is going to be turned into a supermarket car park. I have tried to save it but nobody will listen to me. Please could you come and help? I think everyone will listen to you because you are famous.

Yours sincerely,

Lettice

'Amazing!' cried Ellie May, springing to her feet in an exhilarating shower of letters and tea.

'We'll fly back tomorrow and find Lettice and I'll save her nature reserve. And me and her will go to the *Alien Attack* premiere and tell all the reporters and they'll write about it in their magazines. And then I'll definitely get my SAUSAGE!'

'Goodness,' said Jeffrey, wiping the tea from his glasses. 'That's brilliant!' He gave Ellie May a hug.

'Hooray for me!' beamed Ellie May. 'And hooray for you too, Jeffrey! Cheer up! We've just done our first film together!'

'We have,' smiled Jeffrey. 'The first of many!' He wasn't going to worry about what the stuntman had said. He looked great standing next to Ellie

May. They were perfect together. Weren't they?

Ellie May smiled back.

She wasn't going to worry about what Cassie

Craven had said. Everyone was going to start taking

her seriously. Her plan was absolutely perfect.

Wasn't it?

Chapter Two

Ellie May is Actually a Very Normal Girl, Really

Ellie May sat in her first-class seat, thinking about

saving things. Far below the plane rippled the vast,

mysterious Atlantic Ocean. Beneath the waves lay

shipwrecks full of glittering treasure. Oysters full

of gleaming pearls. Fish full of slimy bits of fish.

And maybe there were a few dolphins, too. Ellie May settled back and wondered, was Cassie Craven down there right now, saving them? Probably, she was. And maybe it was silly to try to rescue a nature reserve, when there was a whole ocean full of other things that needed her help. Was seaweed endangered? Or how about starfish? There was something very nice, thought Ellie May, about a film star saving starfish. And it would look really good on the front of *Giggle*.

'Ellie May, are you even watching that film? Because if you're not, you should turn it off and go to sleep,' said Jeffrey. 'You'll only be jet-lagged tomorrow.'

'No!' cried Ellie May. 'I've got to see how it ends!'

'You know how it ends,' said Jeffrey. 'You're in it.'

'Maybe I've forgotten,' said Ellie May, who could remember it perfectly and wanted to see herself turn into a flying horse. 'You go to sleep, Jeffrey. Don't worry about me.'

'Well . . .' Jeffrey yawned. 'Have you got everything you need?'

'I think so,' said Ellie May. 'I've got my pink cashmere eye mask and my yellow silk pyjamas. And my special noise-cancelling headphones in case I want to be quiet, and my special noise-making headphones in case I want to listen to music. I've got nail varnish in case I want to paint my nails and nail-varnish remover in case I want to take it off again. And I've got magazines to read, in case I get bored of watching films. And a book, in case I get bored of reading magazines. It's called, *Ellie May: Here To Stay!* And . . .'

So when Ellie May slept through the Newton Bingley Hotel's wake-up call the following morning, Jeffrey wasn't really surprised. He had been half expecting her to miss her breakfast, too, although he was a little startled when elevenses, then twelveses, came and went and she hadn't emerged from her room.

He stood by the pond in the hotel garden, a copy of *Giggle* in his hand. Even though the day was bright and sunny, he was feeling a bit glum. The film was finished. The dresses for Ellie May's premiere had been ordered, and the hotel's chef had been given her special recipe for fudge cake.

☆ 32 ☆

Everything was going to plan. But Jeffrey's face was set in a worried frown. His brow was creased into a worried furrow. And his nose was wrinkled into a worried nose.

'Poor Ellie May,' said Jeffrey. 'No wonder she doesn't want to leave her room. It must be embarrassing to have such an unfashionable chaperone. The stuntman said it, and he should know. You must be very clever to have a job where you set yourself on fire.'

He gazed at the pond, and his reflection gazed back. Little round glasses and a brown tweedy jacket. A spotted bow tie. A lily pad. And *Giggle* magazine, Ellie May's face grinning out from the front cover, beneath the headline:

Film's Most ☆ ☆ Fashionable Star

Exclusive Ellie May interview page 32!

'I wonder,' murmured Jeffrey. 'What would a fashionable chaperone wear?'

'Good morning, Jeffrey.' Ellie May appeared in the doorway.

'Sleep well?' asked Jeffrey.

'No. I had a nightmare,' announced Ellie May.

'Oh, no!' cried Jeffrey. 'The one where you forget your lines?'

'No,' said Ellie May.

'The one where you've got a pimple on your chin?'

'No!' said Ellie May.

'The one where you get sacked and they recast your part with Cassie Craven?' asked Jeffrey.

'No,' said Ellie May. 'This was about Lettice.'

Jeffrey stood a little straighter. 'What sort of a nightmare?'

'Oh, you know,' said Ellie May. 'I just dreamt that she didn't like me. That's all.'

'It's probably the jet lag,' said Jeffrey.

'Yes,' said Ellie May. 'I'm not at all worried about meeting Lettice.'

'That's good,' said Jeffrey.

'Not even slightly worried,' said Ellie May.

'I see,' said Jeffrey.

'No, I'm not even the tiniest bit scared about making friends with a girl that I've never ever met before,' quavered Ellie May.

'Mmm,' said Jeffrey.

Ellie May stood at the Newton Bingley School gates, holding Jeffrey's hand. The playground was full of children, laughing and skipping and stealing each other's crisps. School must be over, Ellie May realised. Lettice had finished her assembly tests, or fraction charts, or whatever it was that people did in lessons.

'Oof!' said Jeffrey. 'Don't squeeze so tight! Look, we can still go back to the hotel, if you want.'

'I want that SAUSAGE,' said Ellie May. 'Supposing they give it to someone else? What would I do, Jeffrey? What on earth would I do?'

'Now, stop it,' said Jeffrey. 'I know, let's play

a game. I'm thinking of something. Something beginning with "P".'

'Is it . . . SAUSAGE?' asked Ellie May.

'Beginning with "P",' said Jeffrey.

'Of course. Yes. Um, it's Lettice, isn't it? You're thinking of Lettice! No, wait, that doesn't begin with "P" either. What does begin with "P"? Nothing does. I give up. Let's go back to the hotel.'

'Oh-gosh-wow I can't believe it!' The cry came from a girl about the same age as Ellie May. Her hair hung in glossy curls all down her back, her skin was the sort that didn't know how to make spots and Ellie May was sure her school uniform was designer. 'Are you actually literally Ellie May?

I wrote to you!'

'I actually literally am,' said Ellie May. 'I got your letter and came straight here.'

'Thank goodness!' cried the girl. 'I don't know what I'd have done, otherwise.'

'Oh, that's OK,' smiled Ellie May. 'I like to be helpful. I'm just that sort of person.'

'Amazing!' cried the girl. 'I watched *Lost In The Post* last night. You were so good.'

'No, no,' said Ellie May, even though she knew that she had been very good indeed.

'And oh-gosh-wow I love your sunglasses,' said the girl. 'And your bag. I totally love your bag.'

'And I totally love your name,' said Ellie May.

'It's so unusual.'

'Yes, it is, isn't it?' beamed the girl. 'It's a really unusual name. I mean, it's one of those unusual names that quite a lot of people have, you know, there's three of us in my class, but I think that's what makes it so unusual. Sort of.'

'Well, I really don't think that I've ever heard it before,' said Ellie May.

'You've never heard the name Jess?'

'Wait,' said Ellie May. This was getting complicated. 'You're not Jess. You're Lettice.'

'I'm not Lettice, I'm Jess,' said Jess. 'That's Lettice, over there,' and she pointed to a small girl in an old brown jumper, kneeling down in a pile of

old brown leaves.

'Ah,' said Jeffrey.

'Er,' said Ellie May, 'I'm really sorry, Jess, but it's actually Lettice that I'm looking for.'

'Oh,' said Jess. 'Right. Well, look, take my number anyway. Maybe when you two are done we can go shopping or something. Oh-gosh-wow I love your phone! It's so amazingly funky!'

'Thank you,' said Ellie May, putting Jess's number into her amazingly funky phone. 'And shopping would be lovely. Bye, Jess!'

This was actually very easy, Ellie May decided. She wondered what on earth she had been so worried about. Of course everyone would

☆ 43 ☆

want to be her friend. She was an incredibly famous film star!

Ellie May marched across the playground and tapped the small girl on her small shoulder.

'Here I am!' she said.

The girl jumped up, and turned around. Her jumper was frayed and bobbly. Her face was pale and pointy. And there was something about her gleaming eyes that made Ellie May think of toffees.

'Are you Lettice? I'm Ellie May,' said Ellie May.

'Yes,' said the girl. 'I'm Lettice. Hello, Ellie May. Look what I just found!'

Ellie May stared down in horror. 'You're

holding a worm,' she said.

'It was under those leaves,' explained Lettice. 'It should be in the soil, really. I don't know how it got here. I'm just going to find somewhere to bury it. Back in a bit.' Then, holding the worm in the air like an umbrella that was made of a worm, Lettice set off round the corner.

Ellie May stood watching her go as Jeffrey drew up beside her.

'Everything all right?' he asked.

'Um,' murmured Ellie May. 'She's gone off somewhere. With a worm.'

'I see,' said Jeffrey. 'I think. And, um, what are

you going to do?'

'Wait till she comes back again, I suppose,' whispered Ellie May.

She waited. And waited. And –

'That's better,' said Lettice, coming back around the corner, a little smear of mud on the end of her nose. 'It's always nice, finding a new home for a worm.'

'Mmm,' said Ellie May. 'Mmmmm.'

The sound of Ellie May's voice seemed to stir Lettice from her wormy thoughts. 'So you got my letter,' she said. 'I thought maybe you hadn't.'

'What do you mean?' asked Ellie May.

'I wrote to lots of important people,' said Lettice. 'I wrote to the editor of the *Newton Bingley Herald*, and to the owner of the supermarket. I wrote to the mayor of Newton Bingley, and the deputy mayor of Newton Bingley. And the deputy deputy mayor of Newton Bingley. And when they didn't reply, I wrote to you.'

'Fancy a little place like Newton Bingley having a deputy deputy mayor,' said Jeffrey.

'It's just like *Lost In The Post*,' said Ellie May. 'The bit where my character writes a letter. The one that gets –'

'I haven't seen it,' said Lettice.

'But you saw me in *Hat Box!*' said Ellie May.

Lettice shook her head.

'Or maybe *The Fat Unicorn 2*?' said Ellie May hopefully.

Lettice shook her head.

'Well, obviously you've seen *A Blind Birdwatcher,*' said Ellie May. 'That's been on television and everything.'

'I don't really watch television,' said Lettice.

Ellie May stared. 'You mean, you don't watch *much* television,' she said.

'I don't watch it at all,' said Lettice. 'I think it's boring.'

'Wow,' said Ellie May.

'So, what's it like being a film star, then?' asked Lettice.

'Being an incredibly famous film star,' said Ellie May, 'is totally and completely brilliant!' She smiled at Lettice. 'Everyone knows who I am. I don't go to school. I can have whatever clothes I want, even really expensive ones. And I get my very own chaperone! Lettice, meet Jeffrey.'

'Hello, Lettice,' said Jeffrey, shaking her hand. 'I like your name. I've never heard it before. Has it got anything to do with salad? '

'No, it's from olden times,' said Lettice. 'I like

your bow tie.'

'Now, I know this will sound strange to you,' said Ellie May. 'But I think I should admit that I am actually a very normal girl, really.'

'No you're not,' said Lettice. 'You just said that you wear expensive clothes and everyone in the world knows who you are and you don't go to school and you have a chaperone. There's nothing normal about you at all.'

'I know,' said Ellie May. 'I only say that because you're supposed to, when you're incredibly famous. Otherwise everyone hates you.'

'I don't hate you,' said Lettice.

'And I don't hate you, either,' said Ellie May generously.

'Why would you hate me?' asked Lettice.

'I'm not sure, but anyway, I don't,' said Ellie May, who was starting to find the whole conversation a bit difficult. 'So anyway, the reason I'm here is for us to save your nature reserve. Hooray!'

'Hooray!' cried Jeffrey.

'How?' asked Lettice.

'That,' said Ellie May, 'is a very interesting question. Very interesting indeed. Yes. I have obviously been thinking about it a lot. And. Well.'

'And?' asked Lettice.

'Well?' asked Jeffrey.

'What sort of thing were you thinking of doing, Lettice?' enquired Ellie May.

'How about we go into the supermarket and climb up on the shelves and shout SAVE THE NEWTON BINGLEY NATURE RESERVE,' said Lettice. 'And then when the police come to arrest us you tell them you're a famous film star and you want to save the nature reserve and lots of reporters and photographers come and it's in all the papers and then the supermarket says sorry and they leave the nature reserve alone.'

'Hmm,' said Jeffrey.

'So, your plan is for us to get arrested?' said

Ellie May.

'That's not the whole plan,' said Lettice. 'But it

is a bit of it, yes.'

'Any other ideas?' asked Jeffrey.

'How about we stand outside the supermarket and chain ourselves to the shopping trolleys and shout SAVE THE NEWTON BINGLEY NATURE RESERVE. And then when the police come . . .'

'Um,' said Ellie May, 'that's sort of the getting arrested thing again, isn't it?'

'I don't want you getting arrested, Lettice,' said Jeffrey. 'And it's probably not a good idea for Ellie May, either.'

'Why not?' asked Lettice.

'Because she's an incredibly famous film star,' said Jeffrey. 'It'll be in all the papers.'

'Exactly!' said Lettice.

'It's a great plan, Lettice,' said Ellie May. 'It's almost as good as my plan, which I think is in fact a tiny bit better than yours because in mine nobody goes to jail at all.'

'OK,' said Lettice. 'What's your plan, then?'

'My plan,' said Ellie May confidently, 'my plan is . . . remind me of my plan, Jeffrey.'

'Who's the owner of the reserve?' asked Jeffrey.

'It belongs to my school,' said Lettice. 'They want to sell it to the supermarket.'

'Have you talked to anyone at school about it?' asked Jeffrey.

'I talked to the headmaster,' said Lettice. 'But he didn't seem to care, so . . .'

The smear of mud on the end of Lettice's nose had somehow made its way down to her top lip, where it hung like a tiny moustache. Would Lettice be wearing a mud moustache when she spoke to the reporters at the *Alien Attack* premiere, wondered Ellie May? No. Of course she wouldn't. There was no way she'd turn up to anything that important with her hair straggly and her trousers dirty, wearing a brown jumper all covered with bits of leaf. Not if Ellie May had anything to do with it. Which she would.

'. . . and then I got a detention,' finished Lettice.

'Uh?' said Ellie May.

'You don't care either,' cried Lettice. 'You weren't even listening!'

'That's because of the way you look,' explained Ellie May.

Jeffrey tugged uncomfortably at his bow tie.

'What's wrong with the way I look?' asked Lettice. As she spoke, the smear of mud wibbled, and then dropped down into the bobbles of her jumper.

'Nothing, really,' said Ellie May kindly.

'You look very nice, if the person looking at you is a worm.'

'Oh?' said Lettice.

'It's nothing personal,' said Ellie May. 'Well, it sort of is, actually, but what I mean is that if you're wearing a brown jumper, people just won't take you seriously.'

'Oh,' said Lettice.

Then Ellie May had a brilliant idea!

'What you need, Lettice, is a whole new look.'

'Does she?' said Jeffrey.

'Do I?' said Lettice.

'Yes!' Ellie May gave a little bounce. 'We'll go

and see the headmaster tomorrow, but first, we'll give you a makeover. And not just any makeover. An Ellie Makeover! We'll get you some lovely new clothes and some better shoes. Ooh, and maybe a handbag, too?'

'I thought you said life wasn't just about clothes and shoes and handbags,' frowned Jeffrey.

'And it isn't,' said Ellie May. 'I don't care about them at all any more. These would be for Lettice, which is totally different, because she doesn't care about them either. No one cares about clothes and shoes and handbags at all, and that's why we're going shopping!'

Chapter Three

Ellie May Waves Goodbye to the Old
Lettice Forever

'So, Lettice,' said Jeffrey, as the three of them climbed

into the car. 'Tell us about the nature reserve.'

'It's got frogspawn and beetles and worms,'

said Lettice. 'Lots and lots of worms. And I think

there might be a bees' nest.'

'Bees?' said Jeffrey. 'Is that good?'

'Bees are really good,' said Lettice.

'There's another thing that's good too,' said Ellie May, who found it hard to get excited about things that wanted to sting her, 'and that's makeovers! Everyone loves a makeover.'

'A makeover,' said Jeffrey thoughtfully. He frowned at himself in the driver's mirror. What an unfashionable face he had. 'Yes, that would do it, wouldn't it? A makeover!'

'A makeover,' murmured Lettice.

'Yes!' beamed Ellie May. 'It's time to wave goodbye to the old Lettice forever, and say hello to a brand new you!'

The car rumbled along the road in silence. Or, at least, the three people inside the car were silent. The car was rumbling.

'Shall we play a game?' asked Jeffrey.

'Oooh, yes!' said Ellie May. 'I spy with my little eye something beginning with . . . makeover!'

'Hmm,' said Lettice.

'Hmm?' said Ellie May.

'It's just . . .' Lettice began.

'What?' asked Ellie May sensitively.

'I like the old Lettice,' said Lettice. 'I mean Lettice. I mean me. I don't think I want to wave goodbye to me.'

'Ah,' said Ellie May. 'Well, as soon as you've had your makeover you'll definitely change your mind! We'll buy you loads of make-up and some nice accessories and then we can both get our nails done.'

'Now?' asked Lettice. 'Won't all the shops be shut?'

'Yes, they'll all be shutting soon,' smiled Ellie May. 'To normal people. But that's another nice thing about being an incredibly famous film star. Shops will open up especially for me! So we'll be able to go shopping however late it gets, and try things on for as long as we want and never have to worry about them closing. Isn't that wonderful?'

'Wonderful,' said Lettice faintly, as Jeffrey slowed the car outside an enormous shop. She peered out of the window. 'We're not going in there, are we?'

The department store of Coe, Coe & Co. was very big and very very smart and very very very expensive. The floors were paved with gold and the walls were covered with gold. The chandeliers were gold and the coat hangers were gold and the knives and forks in the café were gold and the carrier bags were made of plastic.

'Of course we're going in there!' cried Ellie May.

'Their clothes are lovely. Their fudge cake is yummy. And we've got to have a cup of Coe, Coe & Co. cocoa.'

The car drew up beside a man in a suit that might have been made of gold but probably wasn't.

'Ellie May,' he said, in a voice that was somewhere between a murmur and a gasp. 'Do come in. I'm Mr Coe. Can I bring you a little something to drink? Or to eat? And won't you stroke one of our puppies?'

'I didn't know you had a pet department,' said Ellie May.

'We don't,' said Mr Coe. 'I asked Mrs Coe to bring these from home. In case you wanted them. Or perhaps you'd like to have a go on my daughter's pony?'

'No, thank you,' said Ellie May politely. 'We're

actually here to give my friend Lettice a makeover.'

'A makeover? How marvellous!' said Mr Coe. 'Quick! Tell the make-up artists! Call the hairdressers! And someone come and take away this pony! Ladies, if you'd like to follow me . . .'

'Come on, you two,' cried Ellie May, and she bounded from the car and ran in through the revolving doors. 'We haven't got all night.'

'I thought you said that they'd stay open for as long as you wanted,' said Lettice.

'I did, yes,' said Ellie May, vanishing into the shop, and then spinning back into view. 'We've got all night. Hooray!'

Lettice and Jeffrey sat on an enormous velvet sofa in the centre of the clothes department. Behind them stood Mr Coe, and behind him stood a crowd of hairdressers and make-up artists. And Ellie May darted from rail to rail gathering armfuls of clothes, like a squirrel gathering nuts, except that the nuts were clothes, and the squirrel was Ellie May.

Clothes! Lovely brilliant wonderful clothes! There was the world's most perfect coat, in her second favourite colour! There was a pair of heels that would go really well with an outfit that she had been thinking of buying last week in LA. And there, the ultimate clutch bag! Just the thing to take to the SAUSAGE awards . . .

'It's all new season,' said Mr Coe.

'It's all very you,' said Jeffrey.

'Would you like me to try any of it on?' asked a small pale girl who was sitting next to Jeffrey on the sofa. Ellie May blinked. Who was she? Oh, yes, Lettice. The girl with the nature reserve. And this was her makeover.

Ellie May unclutched the clutch.

'Try this, this and this,' she said, thrusting a heap of clothes into Lettice's arms. 'And then this, and this, and this and this and these shoes and that scarf and don't forget this hair clip.'

'OK,' said Lettice, turning towards the changing room.

'But not yet!' screeched Ellie May. 'You've got to get your make-up and hair done first.'

Mr Coe snapped his fingers, and the hairdressers and make-up artists surged forwards. Ellie May watched the crowd enveloping Lettice and smiled. It was, she thought, like seeing a butterfly going into its cocoon, ready to turn into a beautiful girl. Or something.

Never had the atmosphere at Coe, Coe & Co. been more electric, except perhaps on 16th March 1882, the day that they had first installed electricity, or on 19th April 1979, when the shop had been struck by lightning. The hairdressers held their breaths. The make-up artists dimmed the lights. Mr Coe started a drumroll on some drums he'd had brought down from the musical instruments department.

And Lettice stood inside the changing room, her brown jumper and school trousers in a heap on the floor. 'What do I do now?' she called.

'You say goodbye to the old you, and then you step out,' commanded Ellie May. 'And we all cheer and maybe you cry a bit from happiness.'

'All right,' said Lettice, giving her outfit one

final tweak, and patting her shining, bouncing hair.

'Goodbye, old me.'

She pushed through the curtain. 'What do you think?'

'Oooh!' cooed the hairdressers and make-up artists.

'Aahh!' swooned Mr Coe.

'Eeee!' exclaimed Jeffrey.

'Um,' said Ellie May.

Lettice hopped from foot to foot.

Her highlighted hair shone. Her eyes stared beneath gleaming lids. The clothes shimmered under the warm department-store lights.

Lettice looked absolutely dreadful.

Her outfit was totally fabulous and totally fashionable and totally, totally wrong. Worse than wrong. It looked weird and bad and embarrassing. The top was too fitted and the straps too thin, the colours too bright and the scarf too scarfy. Lettice's hair swished around her shoulders. It didn't look as though it was attached to Lettice. It looked like a strange stripy wig.

Ellie May's gaze moved to Lettice's eyes. They no longer reminded Ellie May of toffees. Now, they peered from their thick make-up like a pair of miserable pickled onions.

Poor Lettice looked like a bad joke.

'You know what?' said Ellie May brightly. 'I think, maybe, try losing the scarf.'

Lettice obediently disappeared back behind the curtain and returned without the scarf.

'And swap the heels for some flats,' said Ellie May thoughtfully. 'Yes. I think we're getting there. Push your hair back? I'm not totally sure about that shade of blue on you. And let's try some trousers, rather than a skirt.'

'All right,' said Lettice.

'And,' Ellie May thought hard, 'I think something slouchy on top.'

'A jumper?' offered Lettice.

'In a softer colour,' said Ellie May. 'I think you look best in natural shades.'

'A . . . brown . . . jumper?' said Lettice.

'Yes!' cried Ellie May. 'That's exactly it. A brown jumper!'

Lettice vanished once more, and then came pushing back through the curtain.

'How's this?' she asked.

'Ah,' said Jeffrey.

'Yes,' said Mr Coe.

'You look totally and completely perfect,' sighed Ellie May.

'I look exactly the same as I did before,' said Lettice.

'Do you?' Ellie May blinked. 'Yes. Yes, in a

sort of way, I suppose you do. Oh, dear. I'm sorry, Lettice. Maybe it isn't time to say goodbye to the old you just yet.'

'I suppose . . . she didn't have that hair clip in before,' said Jeffrey.

'The hair clip,' repeated Ellie May thoughtfully. 'Yes! And actually, it's the hair clip that makes all the difference!'

'All the difference,' agreed Lettice. 'Thank you, Ellie May.'

'That's all right,' said Ellie May modestly. 'Any time.'

Lettice looked around the empty department

store, and her eyes began to twinkle.

Ellie May wondered what it was that Lettice was seeing. The last time she had worn that expression, she'd been holding a worm. But now, Lettice's hands were worm free. Ellie May was certain of that. She'd checked. Twice.

'You know what would be fun,' said Lettice. 'To run up the down escalator.'

'Really?' said Ellie May.

'I've always wanted to do that,' sighed Lettice. 'To be in a shop in the middle of the night and run up the down escalator. I think that would be brilliant.'

'That's nice,' said Ellie May.

'And then,' continued Lettice, 'I'd go in the lifts and press all the buttons and no one would ever tell me off.'

'Mmm,' said Ellie May.

'And then,' said Lettice, 'I would squirt myself with all the perfume in the perfume department, and go to the bed department and bounce on all the beds.'

'Would you try on all the hats in the hat department?' asked Jeffrey.

'Yes,' said Lettice. 'I would definitely try on all the hats in the hat department. I wonder how many hats I could wear at once?'

'I bet it would be a lot,' said Jeffrey.

'Me too,' said Lettice. 'Of course, I've never been able to do it in a shop full of people.'

'No,' said Jeffrey.

'But since there's no one here except us . . .'

Lettice and Jeffrey exchanged a smile. It was a smile that Ellie May had never seen before. It was *naughty*.

'Race you!' grinned Lettice.

'OK!' said Jeffrey, and then they were off, running up the escalator as fast as they could.

'Come on, Ellie May!' called Jeffrey, as he came

hurtling back down again.

'No, thank you,' said Ellie May. 'I don't think Mr Coe would want us running about in his shop.'

'I've always wanted to do this!' cried Mr Coe, streaking past Ellie May for the escalator. 'Last one on the roof's a total loser!'

The hairdressers and make-up artists grinned and charged after him.

'You too, Ellie May!' called Jeffrey.

'I'm not wearing the right sort of shoes for running about in,' said Ellie May.

'You're wearing trainers,' said Lettice.

'Yes,' Ellie May agreed patiently, 'but not

running trainers. These are shopping trainers. I shouldn't run in them. They're not designed for it.'

Mr Coe snapped his fingers. 'Stop,' he shouted. 'Everybody stop. Ellie May is right. This is not the kind of dignified behaviour that she expects from the employees of Coe, Coe & Co.'

The hairdressers stopped. The make-up artists stopped. Lettice stopped, and Jeffrey boinged off the escalator and stood panting in front of Ellie May.

'Come on,' he gasped. His cheeks were rosy pink and his bow tie was pointing the wrong way. 'It's fun.'

'For you maybe, but . . .' Ellie May hesitated.

'I'm not sure I can run around a shop like that. It's just not me.'

'Oh, go on, Ellie May!' called Lettice.

Jeffrey stared at Ellie May. Then he leaned down and whispered in her ear.

'Do you think you could join in and pretend to have a good time? For Lettice? She looks so happy.'

'I suppose I could do that,' said Ellie May slowly.

'You *are* an actress,' said Jeffrey.

'I'm an incredibly famous award-winning actress,' corrected Ellie May.

'Well, then,' said Jeffrey. 'I won't tell anyone

that you're only pretending.'

'Really?' Ellie May smiled at Jeffrey. 'All right, I'll do my best. For Lettice.' She put one shopping-trainer-clad foot on the escalator . . .

'Oooh!' she cried as she bounced from step to step. 'Lettice! Jeffrey! This is really weird!'

'Are you all right?' asked Jeffrey.

'I think so!' called Ellie May. 'It's quite a good sort of a weird. In fact, it's sort of . . . weirdly . . . amazing!' Normally she had to concentrate quite hard when she was acting. But now, Ellie May found that she was smiling and laughing without even thinking about it. Well, she had won a BRA. This must be why.

'Someone push me!' cried Lettice, who'd climbed into a shopping trolley.

'Someone catch me!' cried Jeffrey, who'd found a trampoline.

'After this, let's go to the café and have a

massively enormous picnic!' called Mr Coe. 'We've got beef burgers and chips and pizzas and sausages and crisps and biscuits and ice cream and cake.'

'I'm going to have a pillow fight,' said Lettice.

'I'm going to wear a dress,' said Jeffrey.

'CAKE!' roared Ellie May.

It was a night that no one at Coe, Coe & Co. would ever forget. By the time the clock struck twelve, there were clothes all over the floor and feathers on the ceiling and the walls were plastered with a mixture of eyeshadow and hat.

'Ellie May,' yawned Lettice, as Jeffrey drove them back to Newton Bingley, 'I was wrong. That was fun after all.'

'It really was,' said Ellie May. 'I only go shopping with stylists and costume people normally. It was brilliant, shopping with you.'

'The girls in my class sometimes go shopping together,' said Lettice. 'But they never invite me. It was brilliant, shopping with you.'

The two girls smiled. It was a sweet, sleepy, I've-just-made-a-friend sort of a smile.

'I'd better go,' said Lettice. 'Here's my house.

Meet you after school tomorrow?'

'Yes, let's go shopping again!' cried Ellie May.

'I think we ought to save the nature reserve,' said Jeffrey.

'The nature reserve,' said Ellie May. 'Oh, yes. Of course. Have a good day at school, Lettice.'

'What will you do all day?' asked Lettice.

'Wait for you, I suppose,' said Ellie May. 'Bye!'

'Bye bye,' said Lettice. She climbed out the car and disappeared into her house.

'That,' said Ellie May, 'was the best night ever. Saving things is brilliant!'

Jeffrey wanted to say that they hadn't actually

saved anything yet. But seeing Ellie May's tired, happy face in the back seat behind him, he decided that it would be better not to.

Chapter Four

Ellie May is Very Experienced at Handling Interviews

Ellie May lay on her bed and stared out of the window. Her suite at the Newton Bingley Hotel had a good view of the school playground. She watched, fascinated, as little groups of girls ran backwards and forwards. Some boys were kicking a football around. How did they know what the rules were? Or what to talk about? Ellie May had been in films where she'd had to play with other children, but she'd always had lines to say. It made everything so much easier.

There was Jess! Ellie May bounced up on her bed and waved, but Jess didn't notice. She was right in the middle of a gang of girls and they were all pointing at a magazine. Was it *Giggle*? Ellie May couldn't tell.

And there, over in another corner, was Lettice, standing on her own, peering at some leaves. There was something a bit miserable about seeing Lettice alone in a busy playground, even if she did look perfectly happy.

Then, just for a moment, Ellie May thought how very much more miserable it was that she was up in her hotel room, watching them from her window. When the bell went, Lettice would go back inside and be with everyone else. But Ellie May would still be in her room, all alone.

'Jeffrey!' howled Ellie May. 'Jeffrey, Jeffrey Jeffrey!'

Jeffrey came bounding in from his room next door. 'What's the matter?' he called. 'Do you need cake? I have cake! Or how about a game? We could play hide-and-seek? Or musical chairs? Or musical hide-and-seek? Or just chairs, if you'd rather. '

'I'm not really in the mood to play chairs,' mumbled Ellie May.

'Are you all right?' asked Jeffrey.

'Yes, yes. I was just thinking about . . . about . . . the *Alien Attack* premiere,' said Ellie May. 'Have any of my dresses started arriving yet?'

'There are four packages waiting downstairs,' said Jeffrey, putting the plate down on the table. 'And there'll be some more coming today.'

'Good, good,' said Ellie May distractedly. Then she looked up. 'Jeffrey. What on earth are you wearing?'

'I got it from Coe, Coe & Co.,' said Jeffrey. 'Mr Coe picked it out for me specially. He said it was the latest thing in fashion. Why are you frowning? Don't you like it?'

Jeffrey was wearing some leather trousers so tight that it was as though his legs had been painted with leather-coloured paint. And his top half sported a great big jumper covered with grey feathers, some of which had broken free and were drifting down around him like bits of fluffy snow that had turned grey for some reason. What with his round little worried face on top, his enormous

feathery body and his
thin leathery legs,
he looked like a
fretful ostrich.

'Jeffrey,' said Ellie May. 'We're about to go and meet a headmaster. We want him to take us seriously and that means we need to wear serious clothes. Like . . . a suit!'

'I haven't got a suit,' said Jeffrey.

'And, come to think of it, the only suit I've got is a swimsuit,' said Ellie May. 'Will that do?'

'Probably not,' said Jeffrey. 'We'll have to go as we are. But it'll be all right.'

Ellie May wondered, for a moment, whether it *would* be all right. Then she shook herself. They were only seeing a headmaster, after all. It wasn't that important. Not like walking the red carpet, or going to an awards ceremony or anything.

'Yes,' said Ellie May. 'I'm sure it'll be fine.' She smiled contentedly, and cut herself an extra-large slice of fudge cake.

Ellie May had been on lots of film sets of schools. They always smelled of fresh paint and sawdust. Newton Bingley School smelled of new carpets and gravy.

'What's the headmaster like?' Jeffrey asked.

'He shouts at me,' said Lettice thoughtfully.

'Why?' asked Ellie May.

'Well,' said Lettice, 'I suppose it's because I sometimes do things that I'm not supposed to do.'

'Why?' asked Ellie May.

'To see what will happen,' said Lettice.

'And what does happen, normally?' asked Jeffrey.

'I get called in to see the headmaster,' said Lettice.

'Hmm,' said Ellie May. 'I think, maybe, you should let me do the talking, Lettice. I'm very experienced at handling interviews. I have been nominated for a SAUSAGE, you know.'

'But this isn't an –' began Lettice.

'Seriously,' said Ellie May, with her most serious smile. Lettice smiled tentatively back. Was that a beetle on her brown, bobbly sleeve? 'You just leave it to me.'

Ellie May was expecting the headmaster of Newton Bingley School to be like the director of a film, and she was very pleased to find that she was right. The headmaster had a big chair exactly like a director's chair, except that it was made of brown leather, not black canvas. He was dressed exactly like a film director, except that film directors usually wore jeans and T-shirts, and the headmaster was wearing a dark grey suit and tie. And he had a voice that was extremely like a film director's, if the film director was English and quite old, although normally they were young and American.

'Hello, Lettice,' said the headmaster. 'This makes a change, doesn't it?' He turned to Jeffrey. 'Last time Lettice was here it was because she'd chained herself to the climbing frame.'

'Was she shouting SAVE THE NEWTON BINGLEY NATURE RESERVE?' asked Jeffrey.

'Why, yes, she was! How did you know?' asked the headmaster.

'Lucky guess,' said Jeffrey.

'Hello,' said the headmaster, shaking Jeffrey's hand. 'Are you –'

'Ellie May's chaperone? Yes, pleased to meet you. I'm Jeffrey.'

'I was actually going to say, are you wearing a costume for something?' said the headmaster. 'But now I can see that you are. Perhaps you're off to a fancy dress competition after this. Good luck! And you're Ellie May. Goodness. You look just like you. Can I get you anything? Anything at all?'

Ellie May knew that she shouldn't behave like a superstar here. 'Oh, nothing much for me,' she said. 'Just a pot of green tea and some fudge cake, please. And I'd love a manicure, if anyone's around.'

'I'm fine, thank you,' said Jeffrey.

'Me too,' said Lettice.

'Right. Green tea, fudge cake and a manicure,' said the headmaster. 'Er, I'm afraid I don't have any of those things.'

'So, the nature reserve,' Lettice began.

'I have to say,' said the headmaster, 'that my wife and daughter are enormous fans of your work, Ellie May. What's your next film?'

'I shouldn't really talk about it,' laughed Ellie May, 'but between you and me, it's called *Alien Attack*. My character's mum is kidnapped by aliens. It all gets a bit scary. But I manage to save her. And also, the world.'

'Amaaazing,' breathed the headmaster.

'Anyway, the nature reserve,' tried Lettice.

'I wonder,' said the headmaster, 'could I get your autograph? For my daughter?'

'Absolutely,' smiled Ellie May, reaching for the pink marker pen she always carried for just such an occasion, and the large stack of photos of herself that she also carried for just such an occasion.

'What's her name?'

'Alison,' said the headmaster.

'The nature reserve . . .?' pleaded Lettice.

'And could I get a quick photo?' asked the headmaster.

'Of course,' said Ellie May, throwing her arm around the headmaster's shoulder and smiling her biggest smile.

'It was so kind of you to come here,' said the headmaster. 'I've never met a real-life film star before. It's been a real privilege.'

'The privilege was all mine,' said Ellie May graciously.

'The nature reserve!' exploded Lettice. 'The nature reserve the nature reserve the nature reserve! We've got to talk about the nature reserve!'

'Oh,' said Ellie May. 'Of course. Lettice tells me that you are selling the nature reserve.'

'Ah, yes,' said the headmaster. 'It's very sad. You see, the school needs money for a new library. And so the easiest thing to do is to sell this small patch of land that we never use anyway. The supermarket's made us a very generous offer.'

'Mmm, that does seem sensible,' nodded Ellie May.

'I'm so glad you agree,' said the headmaster. 'It means a lot, coming from a star like you. Well, this has been fantastic, but I shouldn't keep you any longer. You must be very busy.'

'Extremely busy,' agreed Ellie May. 'Good luck with your library.'

'And good luck with your film,' said the headmaster. 'Bye then.'

Ellie May bounced back into the corridor.

That wasn't so bad! The school didn't feel scary any more. Even the smell of gravy seemed welcoming.

Out in the playground Ellie May turned to Jeffrey and Lettice with her brightest smile.

'There!' she said. 'That went really well, didn't it?'

Chapter Five

Ellie May is Helpful and Kind and Good

Being incredibly famous, Ellie May was used to having people stare at her. They stared at her when she was in the street. They stared at her when she was in the car. They stared at her on the stairs.

So Ellie May didn't normally mind when

people looked at her. Usually, they would whisper to each other, and then one of them would come up and ask for her autograph, or maybe try to take her picture.

But, somehow, Ellie May knew from the way Lettice was staring at her that she didn't want a photo. Or an autograph. Actually, maybe she did want an autograph. Ellie May reached into her bag . . .

'That,' said Lettice, 'was a disaster.'

'Do you think so?' asked Ellie May anxiously. 'I thought it went quite well. I liked the bit where he asked me about my film. I thought I was very good on that.'

'I mean, the nature reserve,' said Lettice.

'The nature reserve? Oh, yes, the nature reserve,' said Ellie May. 'He seemed to have some good ideas about the nature reserve.'

'He's going to sell it!' cried Lettice.

'But, Lettice, he needs the money,' explained Ellie May, 'for the new library.'

'What good is a library,' raged Lettice, 'when all the tadpoles will die because they don't have a home? What good are books when the birds will have nowhere to lay their eggs?'

There was a silence. It started as a small

silence, and then it got bigger and bigger and bigger and bigger.

'*I* know,' said Jeffrey. 'Why don't you take us around the reserve, Lettice? Give us a tour. And we'll have a picnic or something, and work out what to do next? Wouldn't that be nice? I think it would be nice. I bet you'll have all sorts of interesting things to show us, won't you?'

'I have got some lovely caterpillars,' said Lettice.

'Caterpillars?' said Ellie May. 'There's nothing lovely about caterpillars.'

'But butterflies are nice,' said Jeffrey

desperately. 'You like butterflies, Ellie May. They're pretty. And you can't have butterflies without caterpillars.'

'Yes, well,' said Ellie May. 'They have to eat something. I suppose.'

'Eh?' said Jeffrey.

'Weren't you listening to me? I said, butterflies have to eat caterpillars, I suppose,' said Ellie May.

'Actually,' said Lettice, 'caterpillars turn into butterflies.'

'Oh, Lettice,' sighed Ellie May. 'It's really sweet that you think that. But of course they don't. Honestly! You don't know *anything*!'

Lettice turned and stomped off round the corner. Ellie May started after her, and then felt Jeffrey's hand on her shoulder.

Jeffrey shut his eyes for a moment. 'Listen,' he began.

'Yes?' said Ellie May. 'What?'

'Caterpillars do turn into butterflies. They eat and eat and eat and then go into cocoons and hatch out as butterflies.'

'Do they?' muttered Ellie May. 'That's nice.'

'Ellie May,' said Jeffrey, 'you're being a bit . . . well . . .'

'Helpful?' offered Ellie May. 'Kind? Good?'

'Er,' said Jeffrey. 'Well. I just wonder if, maybe, you could be even more kind and good. Than you're already being, I mean.'

'But I'm being amazingly kind and good!' cried Ellie May. 'I just went to see the headmaster! And I asked him to save the nature reserve – well, not straight away, I suppose Lettice is right, we did have to talk about films a bit first, but I didn't do that for long, it was mainly about the nature reserve. I mean, it sort of was, by the end, and anyway the point is that I tried. Isn't it?'

'Look,' said Jeffrey soothingly. 'All I'm saying is, let's do our very best to help Lettice. She can show us around the reserve and then we'll all sit down and have a nice picnic together. With tea. And cake. Yes?'

'All right then,' said Ellie May in a small voice.

They rounded the corner to find Lettice waiting for them. The wind had started to blow, almost as if it knew how upset Lettice was, whipping her hair up around her face in thin, furious tendrils. She looked a bit like a scarecrow. Only much, much scarier.

'Here is my nature reserve,' she said.

'Ah,' said Jeffrey.

Ellie May could see at once why the

headmaster of Newton Bingley School wanted to turn the nature reserve into a car park.

The patch of land was covered with scraggly old grass and squat, spiky bushes. Half-blown dandelions nodded at clumps of scrumpled dock leaves. The side by the brick wall was taken up by a deep bed of stinging nettles, which rippled gently in the chill breeze. And down at the end, in the murky shade beneath a horse chestnut tree, there lay a green puddle of a pond, full of gloopy pondweed.

'It's . . . it's . . .' struggled Ellie May.

'It's an excellent habitat for wildlife,' said Lettice.

'It's . . . it's . . .' mumbled Ellie May.

'It's got a thriving population of weevils,' said Lettice.

'Whereabouts shall we sit?' asked Jeffrey.

'It's not very nice,' said Ellie May.

'What do you mean, "not very nice"?' asked Lettice.

'I thought it would be pretty,' explained Ellie May.

'It doesn't matter whether it's pretty,' said Lettice. 'What matters is that it's full of nature.'

'Oh,' said Ellie May. 'Um. Actually, though, I just wonder whether actually it does matter whether it's pretty. Actually.'

'No,' said Lettice. 'It doesn't.'

'Right,' said Ellie May.

'Good,' said Lettice.

'Who'd like some cake, then?' asked Jeffrey. 'I've got fudge cake for Ellie May, of course, but maybe you'd prefer lemon cake, Lettice? Or I've got a delicious fruit loaf with –'

'It does matter, though,' said Ellie May.

'Not to me,' said Lettice.

'It matters to me,' said Ellie May. 'And it matters to people like the headmaster. I'm sorry Lettice, but I can totally see why he wants to turn it into a car park.'

'Ellie May . . .' began Jeffrey.

Ellie May felt as though she was running down a sort of imaginary hill, faster and faster and faster. And down at the bottom of the hill there was an imaginary lake and if she didn't slow down she'd definitely fall into the water and the lake was dark and cold and full of imaginary sharks. But she just couldn't seem to stop.

'What's more,' said Ellie May, 'I think the headmaster's right. A car park would definitely be nicer than this.'

'Ellie May!' cried Jeffrey.

'You don't know what you're talking about,' said Lettice. 'You think it's all about what something looks like.'

'Looking pretty is important, actually,' said Ellie May. 'People like things that look pretty. If your nature reserve wasn't so boring then maybe the headmaster wouldn't be selling it.'

'Ellie May . . .' howled Jeffrey. Ellie May didn't even hear him.

'I can't believe I came all the way here and did all that work just for this.'

'Work?' said Lettice slowly. 'What work? You haven't done anything. You just went shopping and signed autographs.'

'That IS work, actually!' cried Ellie May. 'You have no idea what it's like being an incredibly famous film star.'

Lettice turned. Then, slowly and deliberately, like a snail, or a slug, or maybe like a girl who is very angry and upset, she walked round the corner and was gone.

Ellie May stood for a moment. Then she turned to Jeffrey. 'I don't understand how that happened,' she said. 'I was trying . . . I thought . . .'

'Were you trying?' asked Jeffrey softly. 'Did you think?'

'Yes!' said Ellie May. 'I mean I . . . er . . . well . . . yes!'

Ellie May wasn't often in a bad mood. As the readers of *Giggle* magazine knew, she was basically a really happy person, who always looked on the bright side and had a smile for everyone. But this afternoon she seemed to have run out of smiles, and if there was a bright side, it was very small, and maybe not that bright really. And it was hidden behind an extremely big dark side.

In fact, readers of *Giggle* magazine probably wouldn't have recognised the girl who now lay crumpled up on her hotel bed in the late afternoon sun, sobbing into the pillows.

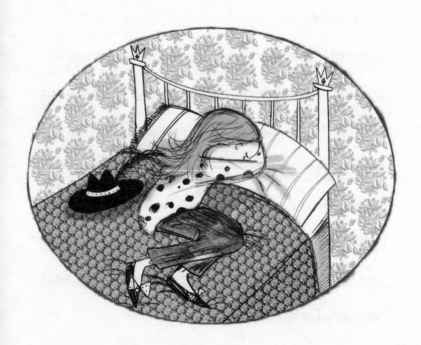

She'd come to Newton Bingley to be taken seriously. She'd thought it would be easy. So how had it all gone so wrong?

Everything was rubbish. Rubbish and hopeless and horrible.

And yet, perhaps there was something she could do, something she could say. There was no way to undo what had just happened. The memory of Lettice's angry face told her that. But maybe, just maybe, there was a way to make everything all right again.

Ellie May sat up. She wiped her eyes and blew her nose. Then she picked up her phone.

'Hello,' she said. 'It's Ellie May here. I'm sorry about what happened. You wrote me a letter and that was really nice of you. I'm definitely going to think about what I can do to help. But in the meantime, how would you like to come to a red-carpet premiere with me? Brilliant. See you tomorrow, Jess!'

Chapter Six

Ellie May Likes Premieres Better Than Anything in the Whole World

'Oh-gosh-wow. Is that the new edition of *Giggle*? It's

not even in the shops yet!'

Soft Newton Bingley rain pattered down

through the mist on to the roof of the Newton

Bingley Hotel, and inside Ellie May sat in her suite

looking at party dresses. It was a calm, sleepy sort of a Saturday. Or at least it would have been, if it wasn't for Ellie May's new friend, who was pinging around the room like a girl-shaped indoor firework.

'I can't believe that I'm actually here!' she cried. 'I know I'm awake because I've been pinching myself and everything but I mean, it's you! Ellie May! And I'm me! And I'm here with you and it's just so amazing!' Jess pinched herself on the arm. 'Ow!'

Ellie May grinned. 'So what shall we wear for the red carpet?' she asked, looking around the hotel room, which was strewn with designer clothes.

'So we're really actually going?' gasped Jess. 'I mean I know you said we were but I didn't totally believe you because it's just too amazing to get to go to a film premiere with THE Ellie May!' She gave her arm another pinch. 'Ow!'

'And I'm so glad I get to go with you!' cried Ellie May. 'It's going to be incredibly fun. I think I like premieres better than anything in the whole world.'

'Me too!' cried Jess.

'But you've never been to one,' said Ellie May.

'I know!' screamed Jess.

'Now,' said Ellie May, 'They've sent me lots

and lots of style options this time, so why don't you

choose first?'

Jess lifted a couple of dresses from the bed

and held them up against herself.

'Where did you get them from?' she asked.

'Designers gave them to me,' said Ellie May.
'When you're an incredibly famous film star you
get free clothes.' She stared at the dresses.

Some were short, some long. Some were slinky and some shiny, some sequinned and some velvety. There were green dresses and blue dresses and yellow dresses and pink dresses and white dresses and red dresses and brown dresses and beige dresses and magenta dresses and mauve dresses and cerise dresses and taupe dresses. Ellie May wasn't totally sure what colour taupe was, even now when she was looking at it, but she was very glad she had been sent a dress in it all the same.

'So I can actually literally wear any of these at all?' gawped Jess.

'Totally and completely,' smiled Ellie May.

'Oooh then I'll have this one this one!' screeched Jess. 'Or maybe this one! Oh definitely this one, it's gorgeous! Or what about this one? Or this or this or this?!'

'That's my nightie,' said Ellie May. 'Do you think perhaps you should sit down for a minute and take some deep breaths? How about a cup of tea and a nice piece of fudge cake?'

'Fudge cake?' sighed Jess. 'You're saying you and me are going to sit down together and eat fudge cake? Oh-gosh-wow that's just the most amazingly incredible thing that has ever ever ever happened to anyone in the history of the entire universe . . .'

The whole of Leicester Square had been closed off for the *Alien Attack* premiere, and the crowd stretched from the front of the cinema right back as far as Ellie May could see. She wondered how long they'd been waiting there, and hoped that her fans hadn't been rained on. Or, if they had, that they'd remembered to bring their special Ellie May umbrellas.

'I can't believe we're actually in an actual limo,' sighed Jess. 'This is so amazingly fun!'

'Are you all right back there, Ellie May?' called Jeffrey. 'You've gone a bit quiet.'

'I'm fine, thank you,' said Ellie May.

'So, to finish the game,' said Jeffrey, 'which animal –'

'I know!' cried Jess.

'I haven't asked the question yet,' said Jeffrey. 'Which animal –'

'IS IT A TIGER?' roared Jess.

'Let me finish the question,' said Jeffrey. 'Ready? OK. Which animal –'

'Oh! We're here! We're actually here!' squeaked Jess. 'And look look look! That's a TV camera, isn't it? Oh-gosh-wow we're going to be on television!'

Jeffrey stopped the limousine at the end of the red carpet, although Ellie May couldn't see it.

There were too many people in the way, clutching cameras and autograph books and microphones.

'E-LLIE-MAY!' chanted the crowd. 'E-LLIE-MAY!'

'Oh-gosh-wow! Oh-gosh-wow!' shrieked Jess, rattling at the limo door.

'E-LLIE-MAY! E-LLIE-MAY!'

Ellie May stepped out on to the red carpet. As the spotlight hit her face, she smiled her biggest smile, and the chants turned into screams.

'ELLIE MAY!'

'OVER HERE, ELLIE MAY!'

'ELLIE MAY! ELLIE MAY! CAN I HAVE YOUR AUTOGRAPH, ELLIE MAY?'

'I LOVE YOU, ELLIE MAY! I LOVE YOOOU!'

The night may have been dark, but on the red carpet everything was bright: the flashing cameras, the sparkling jewellery, the gleaming teeth. Ellie May kept smiling as she walked, even though it made her cheeks ache.

That horrible argument really didn't matter any more, she decided. Jess liked her. In fact, everyone at the premiere wanted to be her friend.

Well, they wanted to stare at her and take her photo and get her to sign things. But that was practically the same. In fact, it was definitely better.

She looked around for Jeffrey. He was staring out across the crowd. And he seemed to be wearing . . . actually, what on earth was he wearing? Had Jeffrey really come to the *Alien Attack* premiere wearing a *skirt*? Where was his tweedy jacket? What had he done with his glasses? And his eyes were darting this way and that, almost as if . . .

Ellie May's heart thumped.

Maybe . . . just maybe . . . Jeffrey was looking for Lettice!

Maybe Lettice was out there in the crowd. Maybe Jeffrey and Lettice had arranged it so that Ellie May would be walking along signing autographs and then suddenly there'd be a muddy pen in a grubby hand, and a soft voice would say 'Could you please write it "To Lettice"' and then she, Ellie May, would write:

To Lettice,
Sorry about everything.
Hope you enjoy Alien Attack!
Ellie May X

Ellie May sidled up to Jeffrey. 'Looking for anyone in particular?' she asked.

'No,' said Jeffrey.

'Not Lettice, then,' said Ellie May.

'Why would Lettice be here?' asked Jeffrey.

'I don't know. I thought you might have arranged it,' said Ellie May. 'As a surprise.'

'I don't think Lettice would want to come here,' said Jeffrey. 'Do you?'

'No,' said Ellie May. 'I suppose not. So what were you looking at, then?'

'Nothing, really,' blinked Jeffrey. 'I'm wearing contact lenses. But I don't think I've got the right ones. I can't see properly. And they really hurt.'

'Oh,' said Ellie May.

'Do you like my sarong?' asked Jeffrey. 'It's the latest thing. Apparently trousers are completely over now.'

'Are they?' frowned Ellie May.

'They are,' said Jeffrey. 'And look!' He stuck one leg out from under the sarong to reveal a bright yellow boot, which started on his foot and went all the way up, past his knee, to the very top of his thigh. 'They're from Japan! What do you think? Do I look good? Do you like them?'

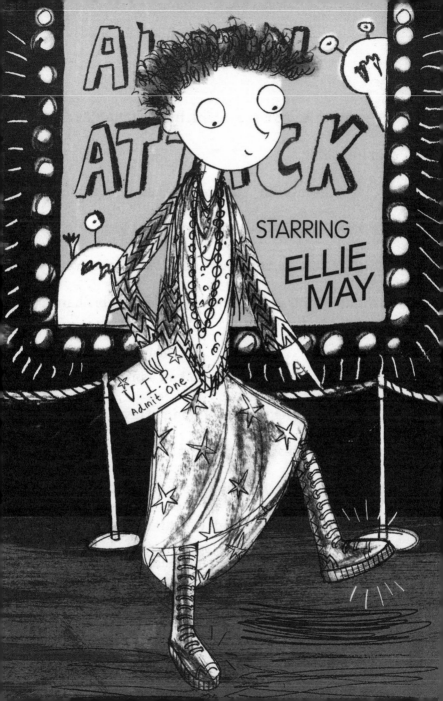

'Er, I'm just going to check that Jess is all right,' said Ellie May.

'I'm here with Ellie May!' Jess was saying to a star-struck little girl wearing an *Alien Attack* T-shirt. 'I was in her hotel room today. We were trying on clothes together. We had a brilliant time!'

Ellie May sighed. She had had a brilliant time, in a way. If having a brilliant time meant feeling all right, but not great, and maybe, for some of it, being a tiny little bit sad. Of course, it wasn't a quarter as brilliant as the time she'd had with Lettice in Coe, Coe & Co. Not even half as brilliant, if a half was less than a quarter, which Ellie May was reasonably sure that it was. But maybe that didn't matter. She and Jess would have an absolutely brilliant time together right now.

'Jess,' said Ellie May, 'is there anything you've always wanted to do? Anything fun? Because now you're with me, you're allowed to do whatever you want.'

'How do you mean?' frowned Jess.

'Um,' Ellie May looked around, and tried to think what Lettice would do at a film premiere. 'Well,' she said. 'We could run around.'

'Run around,' repeated Jess.

'Yes!' said Ellie May. 'Up and down the red carpet. Then we really would have a brilliant time.'

'If you want,' said Jess. 'But we're both wearing high heels. And there are lots of people in the way.'

'Maybe they could join in,' suggested Ellie May, looking at Jeffrey.

'Er . . .' said Jess.

'Or,' said Ellie May, seeing a waiter walk past carrying a tray of food, 'how about we get loads of canapés and have an enormously huge picnic!'

'But we haven't got anywhere to sit,' said Jess. 'And anyway, the film's going to start in a minute.'

'Well, what do you think we should do?' asked Ellie May.

'Oh-gosh-wow is that Cassie Craven?' squeaked Jess. 'It massively is! She's just been nominated for a SAUSAGE, hasn't she? I love what she did with the dolphins! In fact – I'm just going to go and talk to her for a bit. Hey! Cassie!' And Jess scampered away, leaving Ellie May on the red carpet, alone but for an enormous crowd of fans all screaming her name.

Ellie May blinked. She didn't need to have fun with Jess, or with Lettice. No. That wasn't in the least bit important. The important thing was that people started taking her seriously, and for that she didn't need anyone else at all.

The reporters stood in a huddle by the cinema doors. Ellie May gave her dress a tug and fluffed up her hair. She'd flown all the way back to England, and there was no way she was going to let Cassie Craven have that SAUSAGE. *Her* SAUSAGE. She marched towards the cameras as the crowd yelled and the spotlights swung and shone.

'Hello, everyone,' said Ellie May.

'Ellie May! Ellie May! Are you having a good time this evening?'

Ellie May nodded. 'I'm having a wonderful

time,' she said. 'It's great to be here, meeting my amazing fans.'

'Ellie May! Ellie May! Where's your dress from? It's so fabulous!'

'Paris,' said Ellie May. 'But I don't want to talk to you about clothes and shoes and handbags. The old Ellie May, the one obsessed with nail varnish, she's gone.'

'What nail varnish are you wearing right now, Ellie May?'

'Satsuma Sunset,' said Ellie May. 'It matches my hair! But look. I don't care about any of that stuff any more. And you shouldn't either.'

The reporters leaned in. The cameras clicked and flashed.

'So what should we be caring about, Ellie May?'

Ellie May looked down at the ground and wrinkled her forehead. Then she twitched her nostrils a couple of times for good measure. She knew how serious she looked; she'd rehearsed it that morning in the mirror. But even so, she hoped that when this interview came out on television, Jeffrey would remember to record it for her.

'We should be caring about nature,' said Ellie May. 'Nature is really important. We live in an incredible world full of worms and butterflies and trees and flowers and it's all being turned into car parks.'

The reporters nodded.

'So you see, because of that, the car parks and things, I've been doing my very best to help protect all the nature. Because it is so natural. Naturally natural. Yes,' finished Ellie May, who quite wanted to carry on talking, but found that she'd run out of things to say. 'Um, does anyone have any questions?'

'What made you start thinking about nature, Ellie May?'

'I had a letter from a fan, about saving a nature reserve,' said Ellie May. 'Well, she wasn't a fan then. And she's not now, really. But still.'

'You saved a nature reserve, Ellie May?'

'Yes, I did! Sort of. Well, I didn't quite save it, actually,' said Ellie May, who was starting to feel rather strange, like a fizzy drink that had been left open for too long. 'But I tried extremely hard.'

'What did you do, Ellie May?'

'We went to a department store and tried on some clothes and things and then we went to see the headmaster of the school that owns the reserve and that went incredibly well because he told us how they needed to sell it to raise money for a library,' explained Ellie May. 'And it was good, because I got to sign an autograph for his daughter. She's called Alison, by the way. In case you need it. For your magazine articles. About what a serious person I am.'

The reporters had gone quiet.

'So to save this nature reserve you went shopping and signed autographs?'

'Er, yes,' said Ellie May.

'And they're still turning it into a car park?'

'Yes,' said Ellie May. 'They are.'

The reporters stared. And then, one by one, they started to laugh.

They laughed and laughed and laughed.

And the crowd laughed.

And Jess, standing next to Cassie Craven, laughed, even though she hadn't heard any of what had just happened, and was really only laughing because everyone else was.

Ellie May did not laugh. But she pulled her mouth into the shape of a smile. 'Anyway, look,' she said miserably. 'The main thing is, have you seen my shoes? They've got five hundred tiny little crystals stuck to them. Five hundred. Isn't that incredible?'

'Incredible,' agreed the reporters.

'Incredible,' said Ellie May.

Alien Attack was a great success. The audience smiled and screamed and cried and clapped as the giant-sized Ellie May on the cinema screen gazed down at them from her space shuttle.

The normal-sized Ellie May was sitting low in her seat. Lettice would probably have found the film boring, she thought. Maybe it was boring. It wasn't as though Ellie May could remember anything about it, and she'd been watching it for nearly two hours. All she could think of was the disappointment on Jeffrey's face the day before, of Lettice standing angrily in her nature reserve. She'd tried so hard to do the right thing. Or, at least, she'd tried quite hard. Hadn't she?

No. Not really. She hadn't tried at all.

'Ellie May? Ellie May?'

Ellie May turned. It was Jess.

'So, are you coming, then?'

'Coming where?' asked Ellie May vaguely.

'To the *Alien Attack* after-party! Cassie Craven's been telling me about it. They've got ice sculptures in the shape of planets and there's special astronauts' space food to eat and at the end we get given a goody bag. I still can't really believe it. A goody bag.' She pinched herself. 'Ow!'

'Um,' said Ellie May. 'I don't think I'm really in the mood, to be honest.'

'Right. Wow. Do you mind if I go without you?' asked Jess. 'Cassie says her chauffeur can take me back afterwards.'

'Yes, you go,' said Ellie May, who was suddenly feeling very tired. 'I'm really sorry, but I think I'm going to have to go home.'

After the bright lights of the premiere, Ellie May's hotel room felt very dark, and very quiet.

'Night-night then,' said Jeffrey. 'And congratulations. We all thought the film was wonderful.'

'Yes,' said Ellie May. 'Yes.' She sniffed.

'Oh, Ellie May,' said Jeffrey, folding her into a cuddle. 'Come on now. I'm sure you'll be nominated for the SAUSAGE again next year. It's all right.'

'No, it isn't,' whispered Ellie May. 'I've made a mistake. A terrible, awful mistake. And I know it's probably too late. And I know it's the middle of the night, and I've messed everything up, but I think maybe I've thought of a way to say that I'm sorry. Will you help me?'

'If you'll help me get these awful boots off,' said Jeffrey.

Chapter Seven

Ellie May Only Ever Wants to do the Right Thing

'Oh.' Lettice's pale face came peering round the edge of her front door. 'Hello. Where's Ellie May?'

'She's not here,' said Jeffrey. 'It's just me. Hello!'

'Hello,' said Lettice.

'Hello,' said Jeffrey. 'Hello.'

'What on earth are you wearing?' said Lettice.

'It's straight off the catwalk,' said Jeffrey. 'What it is, you see, Lettice, is it's a sort of a coat.'

'It is a *sort* of a coat, I suppose,' said Lettice. 'I've never seen anything like it before.'

'Ah, yes. That'll be because of what it's made of.'

'Which is . . .?' asked Lettice.

'Toilet paper,' said Jeffrey.

'Toilet paper,' repeated Lettice.

'Toilet paper,' nodded Jeffrey.

'Why?' asked Lettice.

'Because that's what's fashionable right now,' said Jeffrey. 'And I've got to roll with the times, haven't I?'

'Ha ha,' said Lettice flatly. She opened the door wide. 'I think, before anyone else sees you, you'd better come in.'

'Wow, Lettice. This is incredible!'

Lettice's bedroom was lined with glass tanks filled with glistening snails and furry spiders. The walls were plastered with posters of beautiful butterflies and not-so-beautiful worms. And down by the window there was an enormous tank filled with sticks and stick insects, although Jeffrey wasn't sure how much inside the tank was insect, and how much was just stick.

'Really?' asked Lettice. 'I didn't think you'd like it.'

'I think it's absolutely wonderful,' said Jeffrey. 'Like living in a zoo. Those beetles are beautiful. What are they called?'

'Mint leaf beetles,' said Lettice.

'Where do you find them?' said Jeffrey.

'Mint leaves,' said Lettice.

'And what do they eat?' said Jeffrey.

'Mint leaves,' said Lettice. She folded her arms.

'I'm sorry,' said Jeffrey. 'About what happened. It was my fault, really.'

'No, it wasn't,' said Lettice.

'No, it wasn't, was it? It was Ellie May's fault,' said Jeffrey. 'But you mustn't think she's a bad person. She only ever wants to do the right thing. It's just, sometimes she gets it wrong. That's all. I hope she didn't upset you too much.'

'Actually, she did,' said Lettice. 'I thought she

was my friend. I thought she was nice.'

'She is!' cried Jeffrey.

'Is she?' asked Lettice. 'Because it doesn't seem like it.'

'She is,' said Jeffrey sadly. 'It's hard for her, being incredibly famous. Everyone treats her like she knows best, even when she doesn't. She's not normal. You said it yourself, when you first met her.'

'I suppose so,' said Lettice. 'I'd forgotten about that.' She squinted at Jeffrey. 'Why are you here?'

'I've come with a message,' said Jeffrey. 'Ellie May wants to talk to you.'

'I don't want to talk to her,' said Lettice.

'Won't you at least listen to what she's got to say?' asked Jeffrey.

'She'll be horrible again,' said Lettice. 'She'll tell me that I'm wearing an ugly jumper. She'll want to put me in high heels and make-up.'

'Ellie May doesn't care what people look like,' said Jeffrey.

'If that's true,' said Lettice slowly, 'then why have you started wearing such strange clothes?'

'I . . .' Jeffrey started to speak and then fell silent.

The mint leaf beetle munched its mint leaf.

The stick insects sat on their sticks.

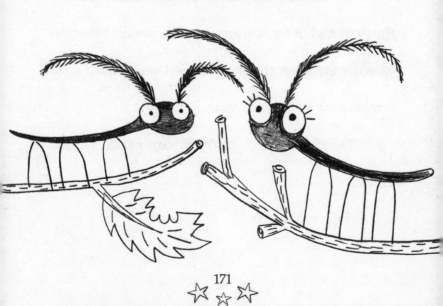

'All right,' said Lettice. 'Where is she?'

'She's waiting for you,' said Jeffrey. 'At the nature reserve.'

The last time Lettice had been to the nature reserve, the path had been overgrown with weeds. Now the weeds were gone and the path had been paved with a wide strip of black tarmac.

'They've turned it into a car park!' wailed Lettice.

They walked on.

'This isn't a car park,' said Lettice. 'There aren't any cars. I don't understand. Has the headmaster sold it to someone else?'

'Ta-da!' cried Jeffrey.

Ahead of them stood a smart red sign, which proclaimed:

WELCOME TO THE NEWTON BINGLEY NATURE RESERVE

At that moment, Ellie May exploded out of a nearby bush.

'Surprise!' she cried. 'I've been waiting in there for ages and ages and ages and I'm completely covered in spiders. There's a big one in my hair right now. It's like having a spider hat. I didn't know that spiders lived in bushes. I thought they lived on webs. Maybe they have webs in bushes. But flies don't fly through bushes, do they? Or maybe they do? Anyway. SURPRISE!'

'I can't believe it,' murmured Lettice.

'Come on, come and look at everything,' said Ellie May, grabbing Lettice and pulling her along.

'Jeffrey and I had our team working all night and all day to get it finished. What do you think?'

The small patch of land was utterly transformed. Where once there had been stinging nettles, now there were spectacular flower beds filled with complicated, exotic flowers. Where before scrubby grass had stood in wilted tufts, now there was a neatly clipped maze. And where there had been a murky green pond, now there glistened a perfect circle of pure blue water. In the centre stood a large gold statue of Lettice standing on one leg, a fountain spouting out of her mouth.

'It's . . . it's . . .' Lettice gaped.

'It's lovely, isn't it?' said Ellie May. 'I made it nice so you can see how sorry I am and maybe you'll like me again and we can be friends. If you want. As the perfect happy ending.'

A bumblebee landed on one of the complicated, exotic flowers. The flower snapped shut and ate it.

'The perfect happy ending,' repeated Ellie May.

A butterfly fluttered by, as though it was looking for a nature reserve but couldn't find one.

'The . . . perfect . . . happy . . . ending?' said Ellie May.

Lettice was staring at the pond. Then she turned to the flowerbed, and from the flowerbed to the maze, and from the maze to the golden statue.

'What have you done?' she said.

'I fixed your nature reserve,' said Ellie May.

'It didn't need fixing,' said Lettice. 'Not everything needs a makeover. Some things are nice just the way they are.'

'But I made it nice for you,' said Ellie May weakly.

'It was nice before,' said Lettice.

'No, it wasn't,' said Ellie May. 'It wasn't very nice at all. It was full of stinging nettles. There weren't really any flowers or anything.'

'It was a good nature reserve before!' cried Lettice. 'There were beetles and snails and frogs and slugs. They didn't mind the stinging nettles. They liked the stinging nettles. I know you didn't like them. But it's a nature reserve. Not an Ellie May reserve.'

'Oh,' said Ellie May.

Lettice stared. Then she said, 'I don't know why you bothered. It's still going to be turned into a car park.'

'No, it isn't,' said Ellie May. 'That's my other news, actually. It's not going to turn into a car park.

Not now, not ever.'

'Why not?' asked Lettice.

'Because I bought it,' said Ellie May. 'For you!'

Lettice flushed bright red. 'You bought it?'

'Yes,' said Ellie May. 'As a sort of a present. A very early birthday present. Or maybe a very late birthday present. When is your birthday, Lettice?'

'So we went to see the headmaster and I had to try on clothes and we had that fight, all for . . . all for nothing?' cried Lettice. 'I've never had an argument like that with anyone. It was horrible.'

'I know,' said Ellie May softly.

'It made me cry,' said Lettice.

'Me too,' whispered Ellie May.

'Then why are you doing this now?' asked Lettice. 'When you could have just bought it when you first got my letter and saved us all that trouble?'

'Because I only thought of it last night!' choked Ellie May. 'After the premiere. I missed you and I went home and I thought about what you'd said, and I tried properly this time. I really did do my very, very best. I'm sorry it wasn't good enough.' She wiped her eyes. 'I'm going away now so you won't ever have to see me again. But I'll get my people to put everything back the way it was. I hope the garden centre sells stinging nettles.'

For once Ellie May didn't look like an incredibly famous film star. Instead, Lettice saw a small, lonely girl, with tears running down her cheeks and a spider on her head.

Lettice hadn't seen Ellie May in *Please Forgive Me*. She hadn't seen her in *The Apology*. And if she'd caught Ellie May's performance in *A Thousand Splendid Sorries*, it had been a long time ago.

Lettice took a deep breath.

'Um,' she said. 'Well, you were right about the flowers, actually. Bees like flowers. Not these flowers. But other flowers might be nice.'

'I'll get rid of the maze,' snuffled Ellie May. 'Now that I think about it properly, a nature reserve doesn't really need a maze. The nature might get lost.'

'No, don't get rid of it,' said Lettice. 'Those

bushes are actually an excellent habitat for insects and birds. We'll let them grow a bit and they'll be brilliant.'

'What about the statue?' asked Ellie May. 'Is that a habitat too?'

'The statue is all right for wildlife,' said Lettice. 'Birds can perch on it. But I would still like to get rid of it. It's a bit embarrassing.'

'Is it?' asked Ellie May.

'It is,' said Lettice. 'But we can keep most of the other things.'

'We?' said Ellie May. 'We?'

'You don't think that this nature reserve is

finished, do you?' said Lettice sternly. 'If you really mean it, about trying properly, then you'll have to get your hands dirty. Not your people. You.'

'Oh!' said Ellie May. 'Yes, I can get my hands dirty. So long as I'm allowed to wash them when I've finished. I am, aren't I?'

'You are allowed to wash your hands when you've finished,' said Lettice. 'But you don't have to. I don't wash my hands very much.'

'It's one of the things that I like most about you,' said Ellie May. 'Which is weird, because if you'd asked me a week ago, I'd have said that I wouldn't like it at all.

Ellie May smiled at Lettice, and Lettice smiled back. It was a small, shy, I-hope-we-can-be-friends-again sort of a smile.

'And if you had asked me a week ago,' said Lettice, 'I'd have said that I wouldn't like someone who wanted to wash their hands all the time. I'm glad I'm not the me I was a week ago any more.'

The I-hope-we-can-be-friends-again smile stretched into an enormous, beamy, we're-definitely-friends-for-ever-and-ever one.

'Now, Lettice,' said Jeffrey, 'I want to see that bees' nest you were telling us about. And those caterpillars.'

'I've been thinking about that, actually,' said Ellie May. 'About butterflies and caterpillars and them being the same thing.'

'Ye-es . . .' said Jeffrey.

'And I was thinking, does that mean that slugs can turn into something else too? Because they're a bit squishy, like caterpillars are, so maybe they grow wings and become moths? I'd like slugs a lot better if they turned into moths. And worms would change into snakes, because they're long. And woodlice could become hedgehogs. Because they both curl up into balls.'

'Ellie May,' said Jeffrey, 'I'm afraid slugs don't

turn into moths.'

'And worms definitely don't turn into snakes,' said Lettice.

'Oh,' said Ellie May. 'That's a shame. A massive shame. Although . . . wait . . . does that mean . . . that woodlice really do turn into hedgehogs? Amazing!'

Chapter Eight

Ellie May is Thinking of a Fudge Cake

'Oh, no! The aliens are back!'

'Cut!' called the director. 'OK, that's a wrap. Great first day's filming, everyone. I think *Alien Attack 2* is going to be an enormous hit.'

The hair stylist put down his comb, the

lighting assistant switched off the lights and the set decorator crumpled up his set decorations and threw them into the bin.

'Good work, Ellie May. That was another fabulous performance,' said the director. 'See you tomorrow. We're shooting the scene with the green goo.'

'Thank you,' said Ellie May. 'See you tomorrow. Jeffrey? Are you there?'

Jeffrey looked down at himself and smiled. It had been hard. He'd considered a snood, a kilt, a marabou-trimmed cape and a purple glittery catsuit. But, finally, he knew; he'd found the perfect outfit. He smoothed his hair, and stepped out from behind the camera.

'Here I am,' he called. 'Ready to go and get changed?'

'Jeffrey!' gasped Ellie May. 'You look . . . you look . . .'

'I look what?' asked Jeffrey.

'Absolutely . . . and totally . . . and entirely . . . and completely . . . w–'

'W-what?' said Jeffrey.

'. . . wonderful!' said Ellie May.

'Really?' said Jeffrey. 'Are you sure? Don't just say that because you think it's what I want to hear!'

'I'm not,' said Ellie May. 'I mean it, I promise. I've never seen you look better.'

'I don't understand,' said the stuntman.

'You look just like you did the last time we saw you,' said the director.

For Jeffrey was wearing a tweedy jacket, glasses, and his favourite spotted bow tie.

'I know he does,' said Ellie May. 'And I'm glad.'

'I do *quite* like feathery jumpers,' said Jeffrey, 'and leather trousers. And thigh boots. Actually, I don't really like thigh boots. But I like tweedy jackets and glasses and spotted bow ties very much indeed.'

'Good,' said Ellie May. 'Because my Jeffrey wears tweedy jackets and glasses and spotted bow ties. And that's the Jeffrey I like best in the whole wide world.'

Back in the trailer, Jeffrey helped Ellie May to wipe off her make-up. 'Before you learn your lines for tomorrow,' he said, 'I've got three nice things for you.'

'Oooh, let's make it a game,' said Ellie May. 'Ummm. Is one of them . . . something to do . . .

with . . . antelopes?'

'None of them are anything to do with antelopes,' said Jeffrey.

'Not antelopes. All right. Hmm. How about . . . fudge cake?' tried Ellie May.

'Yes,' smiled Jeffrey.

'Right. So that leaves two other things,' said Ellie May. 'Um. Is one of them . . . something to do with . . . fudge cake?'

'The two other things aren't to do with fudge cake, no,' said Jeffrey.

'OK. Two things that aren't fudge cake,' said Ellie May. 'Er. Hmm. I literally can't think of anything that isn't a fudge cake. Or antelopes.

Except . . . maybe . . . no. I'm thinking of an antelope

eating a fudge cake.'

'The first other thing is that Lettice has written

to you,' said Jeffrey, handing her the letter.

Dear Ellie May

The nature reserve is getting better and better. There are lots of frogs in the pond and yesterday I found three newts. The flowers we planted are really pretty and they are attracting lots of insects.

The caterpillars did turn into butterflies. Maybe one day the woodlice will turn into hedgehogs too. If they do I will write to you straight away, so that you can tell the scientists like you said.

I hope your film is going well.

Lots of love

Lettice xxx

'That's brilliant!' cried Ellie May. 'I'm so glad.'

'And the other nice thing,' said Jeffrey, 'is that I've got a copy of *Giggle* magazine. If you're interested.'

'Is my interview in there?' asked Ellie May.

'Maybe,' said Jeffrey. 'Why don't you have a look?'

Why We're Taking Ellie May Very Seriously Indeed

So, hands up who thought actress Ellie May was all about clothes and handbags? Yes, us too, but she's shown us how wrong we were.

'I want to congratulate Cassie on winning her SAUSAGE, and ask her if she'd like to come and help me down at the Newton Bingley Nature Reserve,' the charming young lady told us. 'I've been doing

Seriously And Unbelievably Stunningly Amazingest Girl Ever

Giggle

a lot of work there and it's been amazing. I've learned so much. And I've made a new friend, too.'

OO I want to congratulate Cassie on winning her SAUSAGE OO

The new friend is a Newton Bingley resident named Lettice. 'I think everyone ought to be more like her,' Ellie May confided.

'Especially me. So I'm learning about worms and beetles and bees. They may not be pretty or smell nice, but they're really important. We need bees for making honey, and worms for munching up leaves. And we need beetles for, well, I'm still not totally sure why we need beetles but we definitely and completely do.'

'I'm so proud of you,' said Jeffrey. 'Now, time for your cake?'

'Hooray!' cried Ellie May. 'Except. Maybe. If I'm being taken seriously now, I probably shouldn't have fudge cake any more.'

'Why not?' asked Jeffrey.

'Fudge cake isn't the sort of thing that serious people eat,' said Ellie May. 'Serious people eat brown bread and cauliflower. And I should tie my hair back. And I should definitely stop reading *Giggle*.'

Jeffrey shrugged. 'If you say so. Now, get your things together, I'm going to fetch the car. See you in a minute.'

Ellie May went to the mirror, and lifted her hair into a ponytail. Yes. Much more serious. And tomorrow she'd get some cauliflower. But there was one thing she could do right away . . .

She picked up *Giggle*, and went to the dustbin.

And then stopped.

There, on the front, was the headline:

Why Cassie Craven's Wearing Yellow!

Would a serious person read an article like that? Probably not. Definitely not.

But why *was* Cassie Craven wearing yellow?

Ellie May cut herself a large slice of fudge cake.

Then she curled up on the sofa, and began to read.

The End

Takes Her Fan Mail
Very Seriously Indeed...

Dear Ellie May

I have to buy a new dress
for my birthday party.
What colour do you think I
should get?

Lots of love,
Becca X X X

Dear Becca

Thanks for your letter! Birthday parties are brilliant, aren't they? For my last birthday I had a sleepover and we watched my film Birthday Girl. I played a girl who was having a sleepover for her birthday, only secretly she was a monster and in the night she ate all her guests.

I wasn't scared but everyone else was and they made me sleep in the spare room.

I've sent you my autograph, and a couple of spare ones. I thought you could use them as prizes if you're playing games.

Love,
Ellie May

P.S. Green.

Dear Ellie May

I want to start wearing perfume!

What perfume do you wear?

Love and Kisses
Kirsty x

Ellie May

Dear Kirsty

Hello!

Perfume is amazing! I keep telling Jeffrey
that I want to start my own perfume line.
In fact, I made him a tester last week!
I mixed shampoo and rose petals and a
bottle of his aftershave. I will let you know
when it is in the shops but it probably
won't be for a while because I have been
banned from the bathroom cabinet.

I'm sending you my autograph, even
though you forgot to ask for it!

Hugs,

Ellie May

xxx

Dear Ellie May

Normally I like your films a lot.
But Packed Lunch was the worst
film I've ever seen. Magic sandwiches
are stupid and I didn't like your hair.
Please stop making rubbish films and
start making good ones again.

Helen

Ellie May

Dear Helen

I am not sending you my autograph.

Ellie May

Why Cassie Craven's Wearing Yellow!

Cassie Craven's back from saving the dolphins, and last night she was snapped getting off her private jet in a snazzy yellow halterneck dress.

'Swimming with the dolphins was completely magical,' said the SAUSAGE-winning superstar. 'Although they did smell of fish. And one of them bit me. I've actually been thinking that I might start saving something else, now that I know they can defend themselves.'

We caught up with Cassie to let her know how much we love her new look. 'Yes,' she told us, 'I'm very into yellow at the moment.

Because of bananas. I don't know if you've heard, but they're a very fashionable fruit. Unlike apricots. And limes, which are just embarrassing.'

❝ I'm very into yellow at the moment. Because of bananas ❞

We asked Cassie how she felt about being *Giggle* magazine's Seriously And Unbelievably Stunningly Amazingest Girl Ever. 'Oh, right,' she said. 'You know, I'd forgotten all about that!'

Turn to page 68 NOW to find out where Cassie buys her bananas . . . and how YOU can get the fresh look that *Giggle* loves!

EGMONT LUCKY COIN

Our story began over a century ago, when seventeen-year-old Egmont Harald Petersen found a coin in the street.

He was on his way to buy a flyswatter, a small hand-operated printing machine that he then set up in his tiny apartment.

The coin brought him such good luck that today Egmont has offices in over 30 countries around the world. And that lucky coin is still kept at the company's head offices in Denmark.

Marianne Levy

Before she started writing books, Marianne was an actress. Not the incredibly famous sort, though. After graduating from Cambridge University she appeared in a few TV shows and did a bit of comedy on Radio 4. She has been in one film, in which she managed to forget both her lines. Since then, Marianne has written for *The Story of Tracy Beaker*, introduced *America's Next Top Model* and been the voice of a yogurt. She lives in London, and spends her spare time eating cheese and hassling other people's dogs.

Ali Pye

Ali has always wanted to illustrate books, apart from a short time when she was seven-and-a-half and decided that she'd make a good police-dog handler. Luckily for the alsations of Great Britain, Ali stuck (sort of) to plan A and eventually achieved her ambition. On the way, Ali studied fashion communication (this was part of the 'sort of'), which is very useful now she's drawing Ellie May's amazing outfits. Ali lives in London with her husband and children. Her favourite things are Arctic foxes, Chinese food and wearing too much eyeliner.

Starring NOW in a
bookshop near you . . .

And look out for my next
amazingly amazing book!